THE GOLDEN DEER

Maxwell Macmillan International
New York • Oxford • Singapore • Sydney

THE GOLDEN DEER

· Retold by Margaret Hodges ·
Pictures by Daniel San Souci

CHARLES SCRIBNER'S SONS · NEW YORK
Maxwell Macmillan Canada · Toronto

Charles Scribner's Sons Books for Young Readers
Macmillan Publishing Company
866 Third Avenue, New York, NY 10022

Maxwell Macmillan Canada, Inc.
1200 Eglinton Avenue East, Suite 200
Don Mills, Ontario M3C 3N1

First Edition   10 9 8 7 6 5 4 3 2 1
Printed in Hong Kong by South China Printing Company (1988) Ltd.

Library of Congress Cataloging-in-Publication Data
Hodges, Margaret.
    The golden deer / retold by Margaret Hodges ;
illustrated by Daniel San Souci.   p.   cm.
    Summary: Buddha comes to the city of Benares in the form of a golden deer and persuades the king to stop killing all the deer in the area.
    ISBN 0-684-19218-7
    1. Tipitaka.   Suttapitaka.   Khuddakanikāya.   Jātaka.
Nigrodhamigajātaka—Paraphrases, English—Juvenile literature.
2. Jataka stories, English.   [1. Jataka stories.]
I. San Souci, Daniel, ill.   II. Title.
BQ1470.N5522E53 1992   294.3'823—dc20   90-42873

A similar version of The Golden Deer was published in Cricket magazine in 1975.

To Clifton Fadiman
who has applied his wit and wisdom
to the annals of children's literature
and brought joy to younger generations
—M.H.

To Michael and Virginia San Souci
—D.S.S.

In the long-ago days, they say, the Buddha, the holy one, came to Earth many times, in many shapes. In India he came once to the holy city of Benares as a golden deer. This is his story.

Benares had a king who loved to hunt, and who ate meat three times a day. Every day he ordered people from both city and country to go hunting with him. The people thought, This king of ours keeps us from doing our work. Why don't we drive herds of deer inside the walls of the king's park? There he can hunt without troubling us.

They sowed grass and made a pool of fresh water in the king's park.
Then they went into the forest armed with sticks and swords and spears.
Making a great din, they drove two herds of deer into the park and shut
the gate. The frightened deer could not resist.

The people went in a crowd to the king's palace. "Sire," they said,
"your hunting puts a stop to our work. Your huntsmen, your horses, and

your hounds trample and crush our fields of grain. Now we have filled
your park with deer. Hunt in the park."

The king agreed. He looked at the two herds.

Now, one of the herds was headed by a great golden stag called the Branch Deer. The other herd followed a beautiful leader known as the Banyan Deer. He, too, had a golden coat.

The quiet eyes of the Banyan Deer glinted like deep pools warmed
with sun. His horns gleamed like slender branches among the leaves of the
trees. While his herd cropped tender leaves and thick grass, he had always
stood watch, scenting the wind for danger. But when men came from all sides,
the Banyan Deer was helpless. He could only go with his herd into captivity.

All the deer were at the mercy of the king.

The king saw the two golden deer. He said to his cook, "You and I shall hunt within the walls of this park. Each day one of us will shoot until a deer has been killed for the feasting in my palace. But spare the golden ones. They are too beautiful to be killed."

Sometimes the king would ride to the park with his bow and arrows. Sometimes the cook would come with a spear. At first sight of the weapons the deer would dash off, trembling for their lives, but many were wounded each day before one was killed.

At last the Banyan Deer called the herds together and said, "We cannot escape, but let one of us be chosen by lot each day. That one shall go alone to die so that the others will be spared many wounds." And this plan seemed good to all. By the gate in the wall lay a flat stone. Each day a deer was chosen by lot, turn and turn alike from the two herds. The chosen one went to bow his head on the stone and waited to be killed.

One day the lot fell to a young doe in the herd of the Branch Deer.
She went to him and said, "Lord, I will soon give birth to a fawn. Save me.
If I die now, my little one will die before it has a chance to live."

The stag would not help her. "It is fated to be so," he said.

Then the Banyan Deer spoke. "I will take your place." He went to the stone and willingly bowed his head.

There the cook found him and went off to tell the king, who came at
once. He struck the spear from the cook's hand and laid his own hand on
the deer's head.

"You are safe, O golden one. I have said that you shall live."
Then the deer spoke with a human voice, soft and clear. "Lord, I have come in the place of a doe whose little one is not yet born."

When the king heard these words, tears filled his eyes. "They, too,
shall be saved," he promised. "By your act I know that you are the Divine
One. Ask what you will and it is granted."

"Lord, spare all the deer within these walls."

"I will spare them."

"Lord, you have other deer whose herds still run free in other forests."

"They, too, shall live."

"There are four-footed creatures of all kinds who live in fear of men."

"I will protect them."

"And the birds of the air?"
"All shall be saved."

"But what will the fish do, who live in the water?"
"I spare their lives also."

Finally the Banyan Deer said, "Great king, walk in goodness and justice to all your people as long as you live." A few days more he stayed in the park, preaching and teaching in a human voice, and then with his herd he passed into the forest again.

Before long the country people came to the king's courtyard and said,
"The deer are eating our crops, and you have forbidden us to hunt them."

"Begone!" said the king. "Not a man in my kingdom may harm the
deer. I will not break my promise."

When this came to the ears of the Banyan Deer, he called the herds
together and said, "From now on you shall not eat the crops." Then he sent
a message to the people, saying, "From this day forward, you need not

fence your fields. Only tie leaves together to mark the boundaries, and we will not touch your crops." And never was a deer known to trespass on a marked field.

The Wheel of Time rolled on until the end came for Buddha's life as a golden deer. Still bound by the Wheel, he came again and again to Earth in other shapes. In each lifetime he became more kind, more wise, until at last he came as the man who was called the Buddha, preaching and teaching. They say in India that the first sermon he preached was in the deer park near Benares, where once on a time he had been a golden deer.

NOTE ON THE TEXT

The source of this story is No. 12 in *The Jataka, Stories of the Buddha's Former Births*, Book I, translated by various hands under the editorship of E. B. Cowell. Published for the Pali Text Society by Luzac and Company, London, 1895.